GW01018739

For Eleanor

First published in 1993
Copyright © Mark Burgess, 1993

The right of Mark Burgess
to be identified as the Author and the Illustrator of this work
has been asserted by him in accordance with the Copyright,
Designs and Patents Act 1988.

All rights reserved.
No part of this publication may be reproduced, stored in a retrieval
system, or transmitted, in any form or by any means; electronic,
mechanical, photocopying, recording or otherwise, without the
prior permission of J.M. Dent

Typeset by Deltatype Ltd, Ellesmere Port
Printed in Italy
For J.M. Dent
The Orion Publishing Group
Orion House
5 Upper St Martin's Lane
London WC2H 9EA

A catalogue for this book is available from the British Library.

The illustrations for this book were prepared using water colours.

C.A.T. CRUSOE

Mark Burgess

Dent Children's Books
London

Caractacus Algernon Tobias Crusoe,
curious to see something of the world,
arranged to go on a cruise. He packed
up his belongings in a brass-bound
trunk, tucked his special red umbrella
under his arm, and early one Saturday
morning, boarded the *Mariner's Star* for
Billibongo.

Caractacus enjoyed the first few days
of the voyage and had just decided that
the seafaring life was for him when
suddenly he was swept overboard by an
enormous wave.

The wave carried Caractacus
for many miles . . .

. . . before setting him down
on the shore of a desert island.

"Well, this is most inconvenient," said Caractacus, "but no doubt the ship will turn back to look for me."

He walked up and down the beach peering out to sea but the ship did not come back. Soon he began to feel hungry. His watch showed that it was tea-time.

Now Caractacus was a rather spoiled cat. Usually all he had to do was ask and his meals would be brought to him.

Caractacus couldn't see anyone to ask. He shouted and shouted but nobody answered. He began to realize that he would have to find some food for himself.

He tried fishing but the fish just swam away.

Then he found a coconut but it was too hard to crack.

'Oh bother!'' shouted Caractacus, getting cross,
and he threw away his umbrella.

The umbrella stuck in a tree – a banana tree.

What luck, thought Caractacus, he loved bananas. So he had some for tea .

. . . and some more for supper.

That night there was a terrible storm. The wind blew and blew and the rain poured down. Caractacus wished he had a proper roof over his head.

Next day Caractacus built a house using bits and pieces washed up on the beach. It wasn't a very good house and it kept falling down.

Caractacus was looking for some wood to repair the roof when he saw a footprint in the sand. It looked like a mouse footprint – a very LARGE mouse footprint. There were more, lots of them, and they all led over the sand-dunes into the next bay.

Of course a cat is never afraid of mice, even big mice and Caractacus decided to be friendly to them in case they could help him.

He followed the footprints onto the sand-dunes and peeped over a tuft of grass.

Goodness, what LARGE mice! They were stacking pieces of wood around a huge cooking-pot. They looked rather fierce.

"A c-cat is never a-afraid of m-m-mice," muttered Caractacus nervously and he stood up.

"Hello!" he began, but it came out as "Helummp!" because Caractacus Crusoe tripped over a stone and fell headlong into his umbrella.

The umbrella wrapped itself around him and he rolled down the slope towards the giant mice. He looked exactly like a red-hot cannonball hurtling towards them.

"Help! a cannonball!" squealed the mouse leader. "We're under attack. Make for the boat before we're all smidgened into sparks!"

Caractacus went on rolling until he hit the cooking-pot with a "thud" and knocked it over. Feeling a bit dizzy he scrambled out of his umbrella.

"Hey!" he shouted. "Come back!" But the mice were rowing away as fast as they could.

"Are you crazy?" said a voice behind him. Caractacus turned to see a cat struggling out of the cooking-pot.

"Those," said the cat, "are the Mugwumpian Mice of Mornay, feared throughout the seven seas and they were going to have ME for lunch."

"G-g-golly," said Caractacus, his knees knocking.

"Still," the cat continued, "you saved me and I'm grateful. My name's Friday."

"I'm Caractacus Algernon Tobias Crusoe," said Caractacus, feeling a little bemused.

"Those mice will be back, so we'd better get away from here," said Friday briskly. "If only they hadn't broken up my boat. All that's left is the anchor."

"Their cooking-pot is as big as a boat," said Caractacus.

"You're right. That's brilliant!" said Friday. "All we need is a rudder – we can use some of this wood – and a sail . . ." Friday picked up the umbrella.

"What's this?"

"That's my umbrella," replied Caractacus proudly.

"A perfect sail," said Friday. "Right, no time to lose!"

They set to work turning the cooking-pot into a boat. Friday did all the working-out bits and told Caractacus what to do. He held things and tied knots, fetched and carried and huffed and puffed a good deal.

At last everything was ready and they dragged the cooking-pot-boat down to the sea.

It slid smoothly into the water; they climbed in and started
paddling.

Suddenly Caractacus saw the giant mice coming towards them.
They had realized their mistake and wanted their lunch!

"The mice! The m-mice!" shrieked Caractacus.
"We must go faster," yelled Friday, "they're gaining on us."

They paddled as hard as they could but the mouse-boat drew closer and closer. The mice looked furious.

"Ohh! Ohhhh!" cried Caractacus.

"Let's lighten the boat," said Friday. "We'll get rid of the anchor. It's our only hope."

Quickly they untied the anchor and flung it overboard.

But it didn't fall into the sea. The anchor landed with a splintering CRASH right in the middle of the mouse-boat.

"It's sinking! The mouse-boat is sinking!" shouted Caractacus.

The squealing mice tumbled head-over-heels as they tried to get out of the boat before it sank. They swam for the shore and, wet and bedraggled, crawled onto the beach.

"Well, let's hope that's the last we see of them!" said Friday. "Lieutenant Crusoe, set sail westwards for Billibongo and Adventure!"

"Aye, aye Cap'n!" said Caractacus Algernon Tobias Crusoe, feeling as if he'd been a sailor all his life.

As he opened his special red umbrella, the sea breeze blew into it and the two cats sailed away towards the horizon.